Food

La nourriture

lah nooreet-*yoor*

Illustrated by Clare Beaton

Illustré par Clare Beaton

BARRON'S

bread

le pain

leh pah

fruits

les fruits

lay froo-*ee*

egg

l'œuf

lerf

cheese

le fromage

leh fro-*mash*

ice cream

la glace

lah glahs

fruit juice

le jus de fruit

leh joo deh froo-*ee*

cake

le gâteau

leh gah-*toh*

chicken

le poulet

leh poo-*leh*

cookie

le biscuit

leh beesk-*wee*

ham

le jambon

leh shom-*boh*

milk

le lait

leh lay

A simple guide to pronouncing the French words★

- Read this guide as naturally as possible, as if it were English.
- Put stress on the letters in *italics,* e.g. leh gah-*toh.*
- Remember that the final consonants in French generally are silent.

la nourriture	lah nooreet-*yoor*	**food**
le pain	leh pah	**bread**
les fruits	lay froo-*ee*	**fruits**
l'œuf	lerf	**egg**
le fromage	leh fro-*mash*	**cheese**
la glace	lah glahs	**ice cream**
le jus de fruit	leh joo deh froo-*ee*	**fruit juice**
le gâteau	leh gah-*toh*	**cake**
le poulet	leh poo-*leh*	**chicken**
le biscuit	leh beesk-*wee*	**cookie**
le jambon	leh shom-*boh*	**ham**
le lait	leh lay	**milk**

★There are many different guides to pronunciation. Our guide attempts to balance precision with simplicity.

Text and illustrations © Copyright 2003 by B SMALL PUBLISHING, Surrey, England.
First edition for the United States, its Dependencies, Canada, and the
Philippines published in 2003 by Barron's Educational Series, Inc.
All rights reserved. No part of this book may be reproduced in any form, by photostat,
microfilm, xerography, or any other means, or incorporated into any information retrieval
system, electronic or mechanical, without the written permission of the copyright owner.
Address all inquiries to:
Barron's Educational Series, Inc., 250 Wireless Boulevard, Hauppauge, New York 11788 (http://www.barronseduc.com)
ISBN-13: 978-0-7641-2610-9, ISBN-10: 0-7641-2610-5
Library of Congress Control Number 2003101094
Printed in China   9 8 7 6 5 4 3 2